The Berenstain Bears'
BEDTIME BATTLE

It's been a long day
and bedtime has come.
When little bears fight it,
tired grownups succumb.

The Berenstain Bears'

BEDTIME BATTLE

Stan & Jan Berenstain

 **HarperFestival**®
A Division of HarperCollinsPublishers

The Berenstain Bears' Bedtime Battle
Copyright © 2005 by Berenstain Bears, Inc.
HarperCollins®, ☙®, and HarperFestival® are registered trademarks of HarperCollins Publishers Inc. Manufactured in China.
All rights reserved. No part of this book may be used or reproduced in any manner whatsoever without written permission except in the case of brief
quotations embodied in critical articles and reviews. For information address HarperCollins Children's Books, a division of HarperCollins Publishers,
195 Broadway, New York, NY 10007.
www.harperchildrens.com
Library of Congress catalog card number: 2003024200
15 16 SCP 30 29 28 27 26 25
❖

Every morning the members of the
Bear family woke with a smile.

They patiently took turns
with their morning wash-up.

They got through breakfast without
so much as a harsh word.

Things also went well at lunch and dinner.

But as the sun set and the moon rose, a change came over the big tree house down a sunny dirt road deep in Bear Country.

The birds became alert in their nests. The ears of the squirrels perked up. Even the ladybugs decided not to fly away home. By eight o'clock all eyes were on the big tree house.

Why?

Because the great bedtime battle was about to begin!

It began with a simple statement from Papa Bear: "It's eight o'clock, cubs. Time for bed."

"Bedtime already?" said Brother Bear. "Gee, I'm just getting my Jurassic dinosaurs lined up to fight my Cretaceous dinosaurs."

"That's all very well," said Papa. "But quite aside from the fact that they could never have fought because they lived millions of years apart, it happens to be bedtime."

"But nobody goes to bed at eight o'clock anymore," protested Brother. "Besides, I'm older than Sister so I should be allowed to stay up later."

"That's not fair!" said Sister. "It's not my fault that I'm younger than Brother."

"That's enough fussing," said Papa. "Eight o'clock is bedtime and it's eight o'clock. So up to bed we go!"

"Not just yet, dear," said Mama. "Not until they pick up all their toys."

"But Mama," said Sister. "My stuffed animals are all set up for a tea party."

"It's way past tea time," said Mama. "Everything must be picked up and put away—stuffed animals, dinosaurs, *everything*!"

"Okay," said Brother with a sigh.

And ever so slowly Brother and Sister began to pick up their toys.

"Don't look now," said Mama to Papa, "but at the rate they're going, we'll be down here for another hour."

"Hmm," said Papa. "I see what you mean."

"Hey, gang!" he said. "Let's have some fun—a let's-see-how-fast-we-can-pick-up-toys contest!"

But the cubs just kept on picking up toys *ever so slowly*. By the time Papa won the contest, he was exhausted.

"Okay," said Papa. "Now up to bed!"

"Papa?" said Sister.

"Yes?" said Papa.

"Do you remember when we were little and you used to piggyback us upstairs on your back like a horsey?"

"Yes," said Papa. "But you're not so little anymore."

"Please, Papa! Please!" cried Sister.

"If I must," groaned Papa.

"Hi-yo, Papa!" shouted the cubs as they rode upstairs on the back of horsey Papa.

"Less noise, please," shushed Mama. "I just got baby Honey to sleep."

"All right, cubs," said Papa as he reached the top huffing and puffing. "Off with your clothes and into the tub."

"Last one in is a dirty bird!" shouted Brother, as he and Sister ran down the hall throwing off their clothes.

"Tub toys! Tub toys!" shouted the cubs as Mama filled the tub.

"Not so many!" she protested.

"But Brother has five," cried Sister, "and I only have four!"

"Bathtime isn't playtime," said Papa. "Only one toy to a customer."

"Bubble bath! Bubble bath!" cried Sister.

"Papa," said Mama with a sigh. "You do the bubble bath while I get their bathrobes. Just read the instructions on the bottle."

Mama went to the cubs' room, laid out their pajamas, and got their bathrobes.

But when she headed back to the bathroom, a strange sight greeted her eyes.

"Oh my goodness! Papa, what have you done?" cried Mama. The bathroom was filled with thousands and thousands of pink bubbles.

"I just followed the instructions," he said. "I poured in a cupful just as it says."

"But if you'll look more closely," said Mama, "you'll see that it says *cap*ful, not *cup*ful."

After a while the bubbles were gone
and all that was left was a slippery pink goo.
"Be careful, dear," said Mama as she rinsed
the cubs with the shower attachment. "The
floor is quite slippery."

But her warning came too late.

"*A-A-A-I-I-E-E-E*," screamed
Papa as he crashed to the
floor.

Mama helped him up. Then
she rubbed the cubs dry with
a big nubby towel, and they
got into their bathrobes.

"Next stop," said Mama, "brushing your teeth—the ones above, the ones beneath."

"Not that old white toothpaste?" protested Brother. "Nobody uses white toothpaste anymore!"

"Brother's right!" said Sister. "Lizzy Bruin has red-white-and-blue toothpaste!"

"And Cousin Fred has purple toothpaste!" said Brother.

TOOTHPASTE

"However," said Papa, "for the time being . . . we have white toothpaste!" And with that, he squeezed the tube too hard, and a big white snake shot out.

Finally, the cubs were all fresh and clean and in their pajamas and ready for bed.

"All right," said Papa. "Into bed with you! And I don't want any ifs, ands, or buts!"

"But don't you want us to say our prayers?" asked Sister.

"And how about our bedtime story?" said Brother.

"Go ahead. Say your prayers," said Mama.

"By all means," said Papa.

BLESS MAMA , BLESS PAPA , BLESS HONEY BEAR , BLESS LITTLE LADY, BLESS KITTY, BLESS GRIZZLY GRAMPS, BLESS GRIZZLY GRAN . . .

"Here's the bedtime story I want," said Sister.

"*The Three Little Kittens?*" said Brother. "Not that namby-pamby story! Here's a *real* story: *The Three Billy Goats Gruff*!"

"No way!" cried Sister. "That awful troll gives me nightmares."

"Please!" said Mama. "There's no need to fuss. It's very simple. I'll read *The Three Little Kittens* to Sister, and Papa will read *The Three Billy Goats Gruff* to Brother."

So Brother got comfortable on Papa's lap, and Sister got comfortable on Mama's lap. But it had been quite a battle, and as they began to read, Mama's and Papa's eyes started closing. Soon they were fast asleep.

Sister slipped down off Mama's lap. Brother slipped down off Papa's lap. "Look," said Sister. "They fell asleep. What should we do?"

"Let's let them sleep," said Brother. "They need their rest."